Verses
of a
Saddle
Tramp

Gene Skaug

PAGE PUBLISHING, INC.
New York, NY

First originally published by Page Publishing, Inc. 2019

ISBN 978-1-68456-450-7 (Paperback)
ISBN 978-1-68456-451-4 (Digital)

Printed in the United States of America

The good ones, the Zacks', the Redwood Breezes', and Dixie's Rebel that were always there and ready when you needed them.

Contents

We look for two things in this life;
The respect of men, and the adoration of women.
—Gene Skaug

A Little Warning

So you want to be a cowboy
And ride out on the range
Work for a tightfisted rancher
That pays you pocket change

He won't ask anything of you
He wouldn't do himself
But when the going gets tough
He remembers their paperwork on the shelf

He darn sure feeds you good
You get all you want to eat
And from some cancer-eyed cow
Is where he gets your meat

You have quite a string of horses
All sore-footed or sore back
They're a real good bunch of dyers
Considering what they lack

He expects you to be loyal
So you ride for the brand
But when you've had enough
The leaving ain't so grand

So I'll give you a little warning
About riding on the range
It all looks good in western books
But it just pays pocket change

The Personals

I love the personal column
In all the horse magazines
"Wanted—real, live cowboy
Wears skintight blue jeans

Must have tons of money
Wear a big hat, of course
Drive a brand new pickup
Maybe ride a horse

Tall and dark and handsome
College education, to be sure
Fun-loving, young, and wise
His heart must be sweet and pure

Definitely got to be a dancer
And love the great outdoors
Also a great dresser
And associate with boors"

I don't know any cowboys
That could fill that bill
Most all of them are broke
Always have been, always will

Some have a new pickup
But the bank has it too
Tall, dark and handsome
Don't fit no buckaroo

And as for education
It was got in a barroom fight
Or once or twice a year
From a lady of the night

If they want a cowboy dancer
Be careful to be sure
Most I know, when dancing
Appear to be avoiding manure

Now the only one I know
Is modest me, of course
But no lady would be happy
Competing with my horse

The Storm

Above the town of Bodie
Just sitting on a bluff
We let the cows go drifting
When the wind began to huff

We reached for our slickers
Both ol Steve and I
The clouds got dark and gloomy
A—rumbling in the sky

We just sat there laughing
As the rain began to fall
It couldn't get much wetter
Just a summer squall

Then the wind picked up,
The rain, and then the thunder
When the lighting started in
We both began to wonder

It crashed, and flashed
Hitting fifty yards away
It was getting too close
To our worry and dismay

You could smell the sulphur
It was thick in the air
The static of the storm
Was standing up our hair

When another bolt of lightning
Struck close to where we sat
And a little blue spark
Jumped from forehead to hat

Our laughing now was silenced
We didn't speak a word
Just turned around our horses
To stay here seemed absurd

We trotted down the canyon
To look for better cover
Wasn't any need to
The worst of it was over

The summer sun come out again
In the summer sky
I guess it was Him above
Hanging us out to dry

Footwork

Haven't seen the cavvy
Since I seen 'em at the well
Haven't heard the jingle
Of the old bell mare's bell

Hope they're not with the wild ones
And lookin' for a change
Cause long about the springtime
We'll need 'em on this range

Nuthin' could be more demoralizin'
For this old galoot
Than foot-soldiering on the ground
And using a damned calf chute

The Housebroke Cowboy

Most all women want a cowboy
Guess they like their style
But that all wears thin
In just a little while

It probably gets started
When he doesn't wipe his feet
Or stinks up the whole house
With that darned old cigareet

He doesn't do no dishes
Or ever sweep the floors
If it wasn't for his sheepish grin
She'd consider him a boor

He sits around the house a bunch
He seldom ever rides
He's getting kind of portly
Has love handles on his sides

He tries to write some poetry
Just to while away the time
But the words don't come really easy
And its hell to make them rhyme

He doesn't much like work
Unless his ropes involved
So he ain't too motivated
To get a whole lot solved

He cusses that darn feline
For lying on his hat
And shedding all that hair
While smashing it real flat

So the Range Knight's armor isn't shiny
Like it was, not long ago
He dreams, dreams of yesterday
And wishes it still was so

The Outhouse

When he got the urge
He shoulda left his bed
Now he'd hafta hurry
To make the outhouse shed

He only grabbed his hat
And coat and boots, of course
His pants left in the cabin
He showed no remorse

He'd made it to the seat
But it had been a wild race
He never brought a lantern
Knew his way around this place

Now our buckaroo was finished
And heading back through the night
When a pickup load of hunters
Catch him in their light

He'd almost made it
To his cabin door
The people back in town
Could hear those hunters roar

Our buckaroo later admitted
He musta been a sight
Sticking out from under his coat
His legs were ghostly white

So if you hear the story
You can bet it's true
About the late night gallop
Of our "em-bare-assed" buckaroo

The Young'un

He looked the barroom over
Before he came through the door
Saw the weathered old cowboy
So cautiously he crossed the floor

The buckaroo was standing by the bar
Studying the glass in his hand
From under his hat his hair was silver
Eyes like pinpoints, hide wrinkled, tanned

The youngster was looking for a job
Said he'd do most anything
The old-timer looked him over
And fought the urge to grin

The boy was wearing tennis shoes
A wire sticking out from his U-roll-it
Only had one thing in good repair
And that was his Levi jacket

The old man fought the urge again
But the grin turned to a smile
Remembered an old buckaroo that helped
When he was young, back many a mile

Conjecture

Heard of poetic license
And those poet laureate
Guess a cowboy poet
Is a poet lariat

What Do the Angels Play

If I should get to heaven
May the angels play cowboy tunes
I don't want no pop or rock
To get my eardrums ruined

Give me Roy and Gene and Tex
Or the Sons of the pioneers
Maybe Ian Tyson songs
Will make me fight back tears

If I'm lying on a puffy cloud
A winged horse grazing at my feet
Angels playing "Annie Laurie"
Would sure sound awful sweet

I ain't no music critic
But I sure know what I like
It's got to be cowboy music
I loved it since I was a Tyke

If heaven ain't got no sage brush
To make me feel at home
I'd better take some with me
So I'm not tempted to roam

But the main thing is cowboy music
Then I can dream away the time
If heaven ain't got no cowboy music
It'd sure—enuff be a crime

I'm sure the Big Boss has covered that
'Cause there's others like it too
Heavens got to have cowboy music
To soothe that buckaroo crew

It's just west of heaven
Where I hang my hat
So leave me here in Nevada
'Cause I can handle that

Buckaroo Life

Well, there they sit
A tub of dirty dishes
You've got mighty empty pockets
And as many empty wishes

You've got ring-around-the-collar
And around your cuffs, of course
Smeared the length of a sleeve
Is the snot from a distempered horse?

The camp needs a cleaning
Been trying to ignore it
Just looking the other way
You really do abhor it

It got purty cold last night
When the fire went out
You woke up stiff this morning
Maybe got a touch of gout

Don't see there's any glory
In this humble buckaroo life
Though there's plenty of nuisances
Plenty of misery and strife

Better saddle that old gelding
Always makes you feel better
To be horseback again
It helps your mind unfetter

There's that new calf again
Bucking and playing in the sun
That red-tailed hawk's making a dive
Chasing a jackrabbit on the run

Guess buckaroo life ain't so bad
As you give your rope a whirl
Just sometimes in the twilight
You wish you had a girl

The Good Horse

He was born on an April morning
From the first, He was a people horse
His kindness from that day on
Would set his whole life's course

At three He started really easy
Broke out without fuss or fight
At four they started using him
All day, sometimes half the night

He came along real quick
Working a rope, or sorting a cow
A cowboy's full-time partner
Wanting to help somehow

He had made many big circles
Worked in the gate at days end
Willing, obedient, and honest
Wanting a cowboy for a friend

Now, for good service, He's retired
To profit the horse rental man
His coat is rough, ribs showing
Still, he does what he can

Standing, resigned to the rent string
Taking unwitting abuse on a ride
When all he really ever wanted
Was someone to caress his hide

Patty Ann

She said her name was Patty Ann
When she asked me for a dance
Though twenty years my junior
I didn't spurn the chance

She was headed for New Mexico
Down there to Buckaroo
Somewhere out of Farmington
She didn't name the crew

As we went around the dance floor
She held me kinda tight
The next thing our hats bumped
She just smiled, it was all right

She asked for four more dances
I never hesitated once at all
It made me feel real bueno
This late night Impromptu Ball

I was meeting another lady
She'd be coming in real soon
It didn't seem to bother her
We danced to the next tune

When the other girl came in
Patty Ann jumped to leave
I didn't find out 'til later
She was sweeter, I believe

The one who come in then
Turned out to be a flop
She was just passing time
While she waited for a cop

So Patty Ann, if you're out there
And you see this little rhyme
There's an ol' buckaroo in Nevada
Who'd like to share some time

Chief

Ol' Chief died today
I took him to a knoll
With a view of the valley
Heavyhearted, I dug a hole

He'd been a real good dog
I never figured him as great
But for nigh on to ten years
He'd been an honest camp mate

I'm in no hurry to replace him
Not sure I could or should
I know that he'd understand
There was so much he understood

So I'll let some time pass
The memories will soon fade
This ol' man will miss him
His loyalty, I hope, is repaid

Nevada Wind

I rolled out at four this morning
To get the fire goin'
The wind was a whistlin',
A-whippin' and a-blowin'

Nevada horses are extra fast
Least that's what some would say
I know they have to be purty quick
Just to keep up with their hay

My ol' dog scratched the door
Wantin' to get goin'
I wasn't in no hurry
The way the wind was blowin'

Went down to the stackyard
To feed my three caballos
When I forked it to 'em
It went all the way to Taos

My ol' dog went to a post
To relieve his bladder
Indians praised the Rain Dance
When they felt the splatter

]The camp cat's dish blew by
Must of been doing fifty plus
I watched it sail across the yard
'Til it disappeared in dust

There are no trees in Little Valley
Though it doesn't seem quite Hoyle
The reason is the wind, you see
It took them clear to Doyle

They say these Washoe Zephyrs
Are the breathing of a saint
But I call my pickup "Spot"
The wind took most of the paint

The Biker and the Cowboy

"I declare, you're crazy"
The biker said with awe
"You ride them wild broncos
The damnest thing I ever saw"

"You can call me crazy
And I'll set up the drinks
But you hafta hear me out
'Cause this is how I think"

"You ride them bikes with just two wheels
To me that ain't too sane
Your arms are covered with tattoos
That musta caused some pain"

"You wear those heavy leathers
On the hottest summer day
Granted I wear a wild rag and chaps
Though it be the end of May"

"Now we both have our differences
And sure 'nuff have good reason
We don't dress to conform
To the time or season"

"You wear those heavy leathers
Though the weather may be hot
'Cause if you dump that Harley
It'll save your hide a lot"

"Me, I wear this wild rag
Keeps the wind from down my neck
Or keeps the dust out of my lungs
So I'm around to collect my check"

But we both like our fancies
Like my silver and your tattoos
Yours is the way of bikers
And mine of buckaroos

We met some common ground
Now we parted friends
Just takes some understanding
And a little time to spend

He still thinks I'm crazy
I'm not too sure about him
But we're not too far apart
We both try to ride the wind

Towners

I was standing at the bar
In this big casino
Havin' me a ditch
It was in the town of Reno

Down a few stools
A feller starts to mock
Sez "Look at the cowboy"
But his pard gives him a shock

He allows I ain't a cowboy
The words were solemn and true
"My friend," sez he, "what you see
Is a Nevada buckaroo"

I can take the young ones
And their mocking way
But what really irks me
Is what grandmas have to say

They'll gently take ol' Grampa
And give his arm a shake
Saying, "Look at Tom Mix"
It makes me start to bake

Now if I was a hippie
With long hair and sandals and beads
They wouldn't give me any notice
They wouldn't pay me any heed

Or if I was a biker
Leather jacket and tattoos
But I'm not you see
I'm just a buckaroo

Just one thing more
I guess a small confession
I'm not the least ashamed
Of my chosen profession

Sortin' It Out

Now he's over fifty
And he never took a wife
It didn't seem to fit
In this wandering buckaroo life

Never planned ahead
Don't know what he'd do
If the boss decided
He's too old to buckaroo

Never got that ranch
Or that little bunch of cows
Now he's over fifty
Wonderin' if life passed him by somehow

He never played no golf
Or owned a fishing pole
He did his bit of sinning
Figger the devil owns his soul

Ain't no kids to fight over his spurs
When he finally passes on
Or a son to keep his name
When he's dead and gone

Yeah, he's over fifty
Life's better than half gone
Wouldn't do things much different
Maybe try and right some wrongs

If he'd saved his money
Might of bought a place
Lived in town like others
Cussin' the lack of space

Could've worked in town, then also
Punchin' the clock from nine to five
With most of it going to taxes
Barely knowin' he's alive

Now he's over fifty
And he out there on the range
But somehow lookin' back
There ain't all that much he'd change

The Jet Mare

I was packing in the Sierras
A place called Kerrick Corrals
Benny was the corral boss
Joe Poole was there as well

We had a little sorrel mare
Never got much of a start
Had no use since I'd been there
Wasn't doing her part

Benny said, "There are some fellers
Need horses at their camp
Lead her out, ride back
It'll make her blankets damp"

Got the horses to the camp
Made it without a bind
But I'm thinking when I head back
This ol' mare may unwind

I step aboard real careful
Thinkin' this might be my fate
But she lines out real honest
Clear to the Gem Lake gate

I step off and open it
Lead her through, put it back
I'm gonna make good time
With this sorrel hack

I swing on, she falls apart
This much you musta figgered
For a little way I make a ride
She really is hair-triggered

Long about the fifth jump
She lays me out for dead
But thanks by far, to my lucky star
I landed on my head

I heard it crunch on that rock
My head that is, you see
There she goes heading out
But now she looks like three

Sixteen miles to the pack station
Got to shake my ol' head clear
I really might be hurt you know
I feel the grip of fear

I get around to cut her off
There's a narrow in the trail
Now that I've got her, I don't want her
But I'm feeling purty frail

I ease aboard and move her out
She never makes a bobble
Ahead, three miles of granite slicks
My knees began to wobble

Down through the granite
Cross Cherry Creek, up the other side
On into the pack station
It was an uneventful ride

Next day I have a pack trip
I'm not there to see the fun
There'll never be another show
Like she made of that one

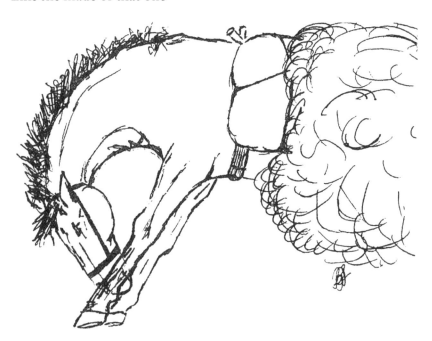

The Forest Service needed cement
Was in the dry-mix form
So they loaded her up, lashed her down
'Twas the starting of the storm

When they flipped the lash rope tail
Up on top of the pack
That sorrel mare gave a whistle
And commenced to untrack

She went across the meadow
Looked like o bucking jet
With dry cement a-foggin'
Don't know if they caught her yet

Frijoles

The frijoles is a lowly bean
That fuels the migrant labor
It's cleared out many a tent, you see
And rattled many a saber

The rancher buys this lowly bean
And thinks his money well spent
Ol' cookie fusses over 'em
But even he can't stand the scent

But the cowboy goes to town
To see his little gal
Better not eat those beans, my friend
Or you'll lose her quick as hell

The cowboy feeds his horse this bean
So his pard will jet propel
But ol' paint began to colic
And his belly starts to swell

When ol' paint has passed this methane gas
It'll stir up quite a breeze
So hang on to your hat, or you'll lose that
And the trees will lose their leaves

The frijole is a lowly bean
That fuels the migrant labor
It's cleared out many a tent, you see
And rattled many a saber

The Old Man

Before the day was over
He knew it was his last ride
The boss man knew it also
As he gently called him aside

"I've got some work down at the ranch
That badly needs some doing
Since I'm not often down there
Things have gone to rack and ruin

"I guess it's not what you like"
As he brushed away a tear
"But you'd be close to town
To visit part of the year"

The boss knew he wouldn't take it
He'd just go into town
It was the only way
To gently let him down

The old man found a hotel
In Reno, maybe Sparks
He spent time in the afternoons
Feeding pigeons in the parks

But he still had a glint in his eye
When he saw the surrounding hills
And dreamed of mustangs running free
And the song the meadowlark trills

He thought the coyote was calling
On that frosty day
They found him where he fell
He'd been seventy-five today

The Awakening

I've chased a lot of rainbows
Although I've never found the gold
I've searched in the Arizona heat
And the Northern Nevada cold

In Oregon I scanned the horizons
Saw Idaho's majestic pines
Traveled the high Sierras
Then California's Coastal Climes

Though I didn't find the gold
It was like the forest for the trees
All was right before me
Waiting for me to see

The gold was in the life
That I chose to lead
For I explored the west
On many a gallant steed

The gold was in the sunrise
And there were other gems
Like the topaz of a lake
Or the crystal of a spring

The emerald of a meadow
The diamonds in the sky
It was there to see
Just for opening up my eyes

After many years of travel
Along hot and dusty trails
I'd finally found the riches
That were there to my avail

Wishin'

Sittin' in a winter camp
Wishin' I had this racket for my own
With my feet up on the stove
Watchin' the calves a-growin'

When I spy a magazine ad
Sez, "Borrow thirty-five grand
Keep as long as you would like
Just pay us when you can"

Now I gits all het up
And writes to this big tycoon
Who wants to loan all this dough?
Least I'll find out purty soon

I'm glad to see some feller
Has recognized my worth
This is what I been lookin' for
Ever since my birth

In a couple of weeks this letter comes
I can't wait to get back to camp
When I get there, I read it
And my ol blues eyes turn damp

It sez, "so very sorry mister
Can't authorize your loan
That good-for-nothin' cow business
Has made a lot of lenders groan

One thing we might add to it
We're not too sure about you
We don't savvy the job title
Busted-up, broke-down, ol' buckaroo"

So tomorrow it's off to Reno
To see the banker man
Maybe he can see fit to loan me
Thirty-five, forty, or even fifty grand

Tough Kingdom

Dust devils playing across the desert floor
The landscape shimmering in the heat
The land of the mustang, coyote, and cowboy
The place of their final retreat

Here because no one else wants it
A desolate setting at its best
Pushed to this barren environ
Known as the great American West

They've learned to weather the elements
They've learned to cope with the worst
To withstand the howling, raw wind
Or the drenching of a sudden cloud burst

They love every rock, every bush
And wouldn't trade it for town
'Cause a cowboy is an optimist
Wearing his hat like a crown

He doesn't know his kingdom
Is shunned by many folks
He just knows he's happy
As he watches the sunset and smokes

The Good Ones

They've packed me over the mountain
Across the alkali flat
Carrying the spade bit
Or hackamore where it sat

Mostly all been good ones
Horses like Redwood Breeze
Or maybe Dixie's Rebel
And Little Donjuli

Paiute Hancock, the Artesian,
Chargin' Johnny, or Pogonip
And there was ol' Sharkey
More than willing to make the trip

Time won't turn back
To where it once has been
But somehow I wish the good ones
Could all be here again

The Sitting

I sat for a group of artists
And one fact came leaping by
They had all managed to catch
The age in my eyes

I know my hair is silver
I earned most everyone
I know that I have crow's feet
From squinting at the sun

My aches and pains remind me
That I'm no youth anymore
Arthritis antagonizes me
And my eyes are dim and poor

But when the artists paint me
I see they paint the truth
They use a vast array of colors
I wish they'd also use some youth

The Buckaroo

You won't see this one
On the silver screen
Maybe glimpse him in town
Looking weathered and lean

From the Rockies to the Sierras
Many horses he's sat
What they call the Great Basin
Is his habitat

He rides a slick-forked saddle
It's a three-quarter rig
He scans the horizons
'Neath a hat that's quite big

A neatly coiled riata
Sixty feet, maybe more
He made it himself
Wasn't bought at a store

His wild-rag blows gently
In the afternoon breeze
A student of nature
From sagebrush to trees

His bit and his spurs
Are both silver mounted
The cattle he's worked
Could never be counted

He comes in all sizes,
All shapes, and all ages
His ancestors and backgrounds
Would fill pages and pages

He's white, black, or red,
Or from south of the border
He knows what his task is
His life's all in order

He handles the cattle
That roam the vast range
And sees the land shrinking
It's all going to change

Buckaroo Epitaph

Let my epitaph read
Here lies a buckaroo
He led a good life
Honest, straight, and true

He never abused his horses
Kept faith with all he met
Had a reverence for women
His dog, a friend, not a pet

He didn't cheat at cards
And always kept his word
Didn't over indulge in whiskey
Was quiet around the herd

Loved what God had touched
From the desert to the peak
Saw life for what it was
A gift for all to seek

So let my epitaph read
Here lies a buckaroo
Let me be remembered
As honest, straight, and true

The Business

Heard about this business
Ever since my youth
As often as I've heard it
It's got to be the truth

How the ranchers are going under
It really is a mess
The economy is terrible
It can't go on like this

Other day the boss came out
Had somethin' he hated to say
But with things as bad as they are
He's gonna hafta cut my pay

He said he was at wit's end
The market is awful slack
Can't afford to keep gas
In his wife's new Cadillac

I didn't know how to answer
Bit my lip and just shut up
Stood there kinda dumbfounded
As he left in his new pickup

Catchin' Air

The smoke was curlin' from his nose
Like vapor from horse's nostrils, flared
He's thinkin' about that near wreck he had
How the Lord, his life had spared

It made his life go stampeding by
He saw it all in a flash
He had to stop and catch his air
After that near fatal crash

He looked his pony over
Didn't seem no worse for wear
And all he could find on himself
His hide had a minor tear

But it sure made him stop and think
Bout this buckaroo life
Why he hadn't settled down
And took him a lovin' wife

There was that gal in Elko
And another one in Burns
Now sittin' here a smoking
His mind it starts to churn

That one down there in Mesquite
An upright Mormon girl
Didn't want no saddle tramp
A-playin' with her curls

That rancher's daughter in Tracy
Was too high-toned for him
Side's her older brother
Might'a popped him on the chin

So he guesses the risks of cowboyin'
Ain't no worse than that of women folk
You might get some bones a busted
And have no money in your poke

You ain't got no insurance
For those near fatal wrecks
But at least you're your own man
Not writin' out mortgage checks

So there'll be other crashes
With the big Rodeer this fall
Best he buys him a ticket
To the doctors' wives benefit ball

Better Left Alone

I'll show him to you
But don't make no noise
If he wanted company
He'd be in town with the boys

See him out there
No, no, way out yonder
Got a good dog buried there
Likes to sit there and ponder

He's a little different all right
Spends a lotta time in that flat
A-straddle that ol' pony
'Neath that beat-up beaver hat

When he came to this country
He had that ol' horse and his dog
They were wolves of the world
And could cut a fat hog

Those days are gone now
His caballo is gettin' older
He's no kid himself
Bad arthritis in one shoulder

Wait, was that a shot?
Son-of-a-mother!
His old horse is down
Oh, no, not another

The Pledge

When I hear the Pledge of Allegiance
The tears well up in my eyes
Or see the Star-Spangled Banner
Waving up there in the skies

I'll probably never be a hero
But I love the red, white, and blue
Because God and this country
Gave me a chance to buckaroo

I have freedom of choice in this country
To work and play as I will
I've chosen to be a cowboy
And ride the distant hill

If I should ever have a son
I'd like him to buckaroo
But he'll still have a choice
Under the red, white, and blue

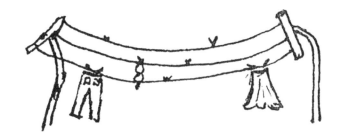

Gary and Ol' Suze

Gary was an Arizona cowboy
He called his girl Ol' Suze
Which had more wit and humor
It'd be purty hard to choose

Gary loved to tell a story
Funny, but true just the same
Ol' Suze loved to rib Gary
That was her favorite game

Their car was named Ol' Purp
For the color of its paint
Talk about bright purple
'Twas enough to make you faint

Someday I'll look 'em up
To have a few more chuckles
But I won't ride in Ol Purp
I've had enough white knuckles

The Encounter

I was soaking in a hot spring
In all my nekkid glory
When I heard the leaves a-rustlin'
And at once began to worry

She came walkin' straight to me
Though a little delicate and shy
Her legs were long and slender
She gazed from deep brown eyes

Now me, I'm just a cowboy
Unused to a female's stare
I couldn't reach my clothes
But sat there totally bare

My heart was hardly beating
My breath, I tried to hold
Her grace was as a picture
She wasn't forward, wasn't bold

The beauty of the moment
Was beauty beyond belief
It happened so naturally
Without fore thought, without grief

What I saw on that day
I never will forget
She even brought twin fawns
My memory cherishes it yet

Memories

Last night I ran a fever
In this camp of mine
Was feelin' awful poorly
Got to thinkin' about dyin'

And while I was a shiverin'
In this hallucinatory state
My mind, it got to wanderin'
Over things past, and of late

How I started out in Oregon
Buckaroo country to be sure
When I worked out of Paulina
Or rode the south fork of the Malheur

Then I packed in the Sierras
For a feller I'm sure you knew
He was Reno Sardella
And he showed me how to shoe

Met a trainer in Nevada
Don Rapp was his name
And because of his help
I learned the cow horse game

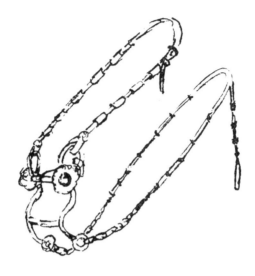

I learned of Spades and Hackamores
The California way
Of horses that spin and slide
And work a cow all day

Next, to old Arizona
Right down on the border
Didn't stay there very long
It wasn't made to order

Back to Reno in Nevada
And the spaces that I love
Twenty-four hour days and nights
And the casino lights above

On to southern California
Mission Viejo for a while
Then two years on the Irvine
It was more my style

Nine-mile cow camp
And the Burkham on Mono Lake
With the sun a-settin' on it
But the gnat's was hard to take

Winter rains in the San Joaquin
Jim Lowrance ran the crew
And for a fork-ed camp mate
Of bones sure would do

Now back here in Nevada
In a camp on the DC Bar
I'm sittin' here and ponderin'
How I ever came this far

I've had my share of memories
Companions, tested and true
Rode some real good ponies
Knew a good dog or two

So if this fever takes me
I know I've had the best
In friends and dogs and horses
They sure did pass the test

Dirty Ernie

They called him Dirty Ernie
For the condition he was in
He's one thought soap and water
Was for sure a mortal sin

He had a camp on Swamp Creek
Up there purty high
He hollered me in one day
As I come ridin' by

He said that lunch was ready
That I was just on time
And if I didn't eat with him
It'd shore 'nuff be a crime

So I tied my pony up
And ventured into this shack
Just then I lost my appetite
I allows I ain't goin back

I begged off on lunch just then
The flies were awful thick
Said I'd set and jaw with him
But I'd had lunch back up the crick

He had my curiosity
We talked of many things
Bout the trials and tribulations
And the woes that life can bring

The sun was headed downward
As I started for the ranch
But in meetin' Dirty Ernie
I was glad I got the chance

In town a few weeks later
Who should I chance to meet?
If it ain't old Dirty Ernie
Comes a walkin' down the street

He sez, "Let's hit this bar
And shoot a game of pool"
We weren't too awful handy
We shot like a pair of fools

I'd just managed to edge him
He shot like he was lame
In a disgruntled voice, he sez
"This ain't no buckaroo game"

Sometimes I think about him
Wonderin' where he might be
In our faster world today
He's a character you'll seldom see

The Letter

When it's winter in Nevada
I'll be thinking of you
Sitting 'neath the coal-oil light
I'll pen a poem or two

Might be about our love affair
That really never got started
And how I left one afternoon
Dismal, blue, and broken-hearted

On the other hand, it might be
About my life out here
How winter nights are long and dark
Wishing that you were near

Could be about my rambling
And my footloose life
But I guess it doesn't matter
Now you're someone else's wife

The Last Payment

I can speak from experience
I've witnessed many things
At times riding a ridgetop
I feel God has given me wings

So when my time has come
And my soul is heaven bound
Take my carcass to the prairie
Then lay it on the ground

That the coyotes and the buzzards
Might have a glorious feast
On this earth I'll have done some good
Filling the belly of the beast

Cause I've spent my time on earth
Taking and not giving back
So carry me to the prairie
In an old gunny sack

If the maker rejects my soul
The devil will have his turn
But my carcass can feed the flowers
While my spirit eternally burns

Ode to the Teachers

Mister Eakins, Mrs. Fleetwood
Teachers of my youth
Doing their level best
Teaching wisdom and the Truth

Teachers of the old school
With knowledge to impart
Yes, it was all but wasted
On a buckaroo at heart

I didn't want Joyce Kilmer
With his poem about a tree,
But out here with the mustang
And coyote, running free

So that's where I've gone
To this arid land
With the wind whipping
And blowing the desert sand

Oh, I wouldn't trade places
With the folks in town
But I surely hope my teachers
Didn't think I let them down

The Price of Buckarooing

I crawl into the bed at night
And lay there countin' aches
This cowboy life is tough, you know
A darn sure heavy toll, it takes

An arthritic shoulder
From a wreck on the race track
Shoe'in too many horses
Has caught up with my back

My ankles sound like ratchets
From trottin' too many miles
I know that my hemorrhoids are caused
From broncs that bucked with style

Maybe countin' these afflictions
Is better than countin' sheep
Cause if I had to stoop that low
I'd rather do without sleep

I ain't one to complain you know
Though I toss and turn and curse
I know that there are fellas out there
That darn sure have it worse

It's handy I ain't homeless
Like so many people are
For this I should be thankful
And praise my lucky star

So now this poem is over
Cause I'm starting' too fall asleep
I don't wanna press my luck
And end up counting sheep

Patience

While you ran in to get a cup of hot coffee and warm up a bit, the old horse you tied up is out there is waiting with—patience

Even though you fed the old dog heavy before you went to town, you know he won't eat till you get back so he's sitting there waiting with—patience

That poker dealer in the Gentlemen's Recreation room knows you won't get back to town for a month or two so he is sitting and waiting with—patience

The banker knows you're a long way from town so he might as well wait on your truck payment with—patience

Your girl knows you're a long ways from town and probably won't be back for some time so she might as well wait with—the poker dealer or the banker—her name is—Patience

Cowboy Dirge

I dreamed of being a cowboy
Guess I attained that goal
But now I feel like a bobcat
Cornered, treed, up a pole

The artists paint my picture
The tourists snap it too
They all want a likeness
Of an old time buckaroo

When I was a kid they said
"They don't need cowboys anymore"
Thank God that they were wrong
Though I'm old, and stiff, and sore

Jobs are getting scarce
Me, I'm getting lean
Now I'm just a misfit
No longer in the scheme

The ranches are subdivisions
There's an abundance of cement
Now in a run-down hotel
I can barely make the rent

My ponies are out to pasture
My dog has lived out his days
I know my time is done
But I'm glad I passed this way

The Survivor

In a Los Angeles garbage dump
Or a rocky draw in the Great Basin
Stalking a careless alley cat
Maybe a prairie dog he's chasin'
But he's a survivor

The sheep man calls him a curse
The cowman shows him no respect
The hunter and trapper pursue him
Never stopping to reflect
That he's a survivor

With man's progress and infringement
This wily creature learned to cope
An example to other loners
He somehow has given them hope
He's a survivor

The Indian calls him Wise Brother
You'll hear him call for his mate
From a distant hill or barranca
To overcome is the coyote's fate
Yes, he's a survivor

Rockwell Painting

Straight from a Rockwell painting
Freckles across his nose
A shock of carrot red hair
Norman would've liked him to pose

He conjures up images
Of slingshots, frogs, and string
A pocketful of marbles
Fishing pole and others things

He's a worry to his mother
As every boy can be
He's really an angel without wings
But not short on deviltry

Eight is an age that comes once
A young man, he'll be too soon
Facing the rushing world
Maybe exploring the moon

So, Nick, take this time
Be a boy while you can
Because the time will come
When you have to be a man

Manhood is a good thing
It has its moments of joy
But somewhere deep down inside
Save back a little bit of boy

Fork in the Trail

"You think more of that dog!"
It was stated like a fact
I just kept on pettin' him
Didn't even answer back

That was a few years ago
Short time later, the divorce
Ever since that time
It's just me, the dog, and my horse

Guess I've never looked back
Can't say she did either
Don't feel any real remorse
Probably did each other a favor

I still got that ol' dog
"Chief" is his given name
I'm still just pettin' him
Wonder who's pettin' that dame

The Indian

This once proud and noble breed
Used to rule this land
Now on a street corner
A bottle in his hand

He never claimed to own it
The land he felt was to borrow
Then the government came along
To show him a new tomorrow

They gave him a new life
Never more to be free
Washington civilized him
Even got smallpox and VD

The government now pays him
For what they really stole
It's small wonder he's a derelict
And lost sight of his goal

The Rock

There's a rock out in the corral
Just a waitin' for me
I broke the danged old pick
Tryin' to dig it free

When I run those colts in
I hope that they'll be kind
I don't want that rock
A slammin' my behind

If I had some powder
I'd blow it all to hell
But that would leave a crater
And I ain't sure that would sell

So I guess I'll take my chances
And hope that they don't buck
Cause that rock'll go to chasin' me
If I know about my luck

It's right there in the center
But it'll move to where I land
I'd much prefer my buttocks
A-hittin' in the sand

Might as well get started
I know that I've faced worse
Like droughts and heat and blizzards
That could make a sane man curse

But it makes me kinda timid
This rock out in the corral
If my head should find it
Just bury me, old pal

The spurs get rusty
The horses get old
But a true, true love
Never grows cold

Buckaroo Prayer

O Lord, God in heaven
I have a lot to thank You for
Of mountain peaks, and rushing creeks
and the sun on the valley floor

I've seen Huckleberry Lake,
Cow Meadow, and Cherry Creek,
Cow's in Laguna Canyon
And mist on Saddleback Peak

The time up out of Alturas
Riding that boggy slough
If it hadn't been for Your Grace
We'd of never made it through

The wind was whippin' at our bock
The snow going down our neck
When that cow went out of sight
It had the makin's of a wreck

But You were there beside me
Just in time I saw the hole
And in that same split second
I know you saw my soul

I know my ways are lacking
Tend to call in time of need
But when I hear the meadowlark
It makes me stop and heed

I hear the coyote calling
From a distant hill
He probably doesn't need Your help
Me, I always will

Don't often think of You
Though I know I should
'Til I see the stars at night
Or an elk out in the wood

I've been to Harney County
Up there out of Burns
Down to Arivaca
Where vaqueros take theirs turns

From the San Joaquin to the Walker River
A restless drifter I've been
But with Your strength, at arm's length
I'd do it all again

You've helped me along in life
Though again I'm bound to fail
But if I get lost, battered and tossed
You'll nudge me back on to the trail
Amen

About the Author

Raised on a rock pile on the banks of Oregon's North Santiam River, Gene's all-consuming interest was animals and nature. He has been involved in the livestock industry in one form or another for close to thirty years, starting out buckarooing (cowboying) in Eastern Oregon in the early sixties before moving to Reno, Nevada, where he set up his own training stables at the age of twenty-three in 1965.

In the seventies, the author was called back to the buckaroo life where he has been ever since, except for four years he spent handling the horses and lion in the stage show, "Hello Hollywood, Hello," along with some modeling and a minor part in the movie Desert Hearts.

CPSIA information can be obtained
at www.ICGtesting.com
Printed in the USA
LVHW091041301219
642041LV00005B/846/P